George Meredith

Ballads and Poems of Tragic Life

George Meredith

Ballads and Poems of Tragic Life

ISBN/EAN: 9783744791984

Printed in Europe, USA, Canada, Australia, Japan

Cover: Foto ©Andreas Hilbeck / pixelio.de

More available books at **www.hansebooks.com**

BY GEORGE MEREDITH.

BALLADS AND POEMS OF TRAGIC LIFE. Globe 8vo. 6s.

POEMS AND LYRICS OF THE JOY OF EARTH. Globe 8vo. 6s.

A READING OF EARTH. Globe 8vo. 5s.

MODERN LOVE : A Reprint. To which is added, THE SAGE ENAMOURED AND THE HONEST LADY. Globe 8vo. 5s.

POEMS : THE EMPTY PURSE, together with ODES TO THE COMIC SPIRIT, TO YOUTH IN MEMORY, AND VERSES. Fcap. 8vo. 5s.

MACMILLAN AND CO., LONDON.

BALLADS AND POEMS

OF

TRAGIC LIFE

BALLADS AND POEMS

OF

TRAGIC LIFE

BY

GEORGE MEREDITH

London

MACMILLAN AND CO.

AND NEW YORK

1894

First Edition 1887. *Second Edition* 1894

CONTENTS

THE TWO MASKS

MELPOMENE among her livid people,

Ere stroke of lyre, upon Thaleia looks,

Warned by old contests that one museful ripple

Along those lips of rose with tendril hooks,

Forebodes disturbance in the springs of pathos,

Perchance may change of masks midway demand,

Albeit the man rise mountainous as Athos,

The woman wild as Cape Leucadia stand.

T   B

II.

For this the Comic Muse exacts of creatures

Appealing to the fount of tears : that they

Strive never to outleap our human features,

And do Right Reason's ordinance obey,

In peril of the hum to laughter nighest.

But prove they under stress of action's fire

Nobleness, to that test of Reason highest,

She bows : she waves them for the loftier lyre.

ARCHDUCHESS ANNE

I.

I.

In middle age an evil thing
  Befel Archduchess Anne :
She looked outside her wedding-ring
  Upon a princely man.

II.

Count Louis was for horse and arms ;
  And if its beacon waved,
For love ; but ladies had not charms
  To match a danger braved.

III.

On battlefields he was the bow

Bestrung to fly the shaft :

In idle hours his heart would flow

As winds on currents waft.

IV.

His blood was of those warrior tribes

That streamed from morning's fire,

Whom now with traps and now with bribes

The wily Council wire.

V.

Archduchess Anne the Council ruled,

Count Louis his great dame ;

And woe to both when one had cooled !

Little was she to blame.

VI.

Among her chiefs who spun their plots,

Old Kraken stood the sword :

As sharp his wits for cutting knots

Of babble he abhorred.

VII.

He reverenced her name and line,

  Nor other merit had

Save soldierwise to wait her sign,

  And do the deed she bade.

VIII.

He saw her hand jump at her side

  Ere royally she smiled

On Louis and his fair young bride

  Where courtly ranks defiled.

IX.

That was a moment when a shock

  Through the procession ran,

And thrilled the plumes, and stayed the clock,

  Yet smiled Archduchess Anne.

X.

No touch gave she to hound in leash,

  No wink to sword in sheath :

She seemed a woman scarce of flesh ;

  Above it, or beneath.

XI.

Old Kraken spied with kennelled snarl,

His Lady deemed disgraced.

He footed as on burning marl,

When out of Hall he paced.

XII.

'Twas seen he hammered striding legs,

And stopped, and strode again.

Now Vengeance has a brood of eggs,

But Patience must be hen.

XIII.

Too slow are they for wrath to hatch,

Too hot for time to rear.

Old Kraken kept unwinking watch ;

He marked his day appear.

XIV.

He neighed a laugh, though moods were rough

With standards in revolt :

His nostrils took the news for snuff,

His smacking lips for salt.

XV.

Count Louis' wavy cock's plumes led

His troops of black-haired manes,

A rebel; and old Kraken sped

To front him on the plains.

XVI.

Then camp opposed to camp did they

Fret earth with panther claws

For signal of a bloody day,

Each reading from the Laws.

XVII.

'Forefend it, heaven!' Count Louis cried,

'And let the righteous plead:

My country is a willing bride,

Was never slave decreed.

XVIII.

'Not we for thirst of blood appeal

To sword and slaughter curst;

We have God's blessing on our steel,

Do we our pleading first.'

XIX.

Count Louis, soul of chivalry,

    Put trust in plighted word ;

By starlight on the broad brown lea,

    To bar the strife he spurred.

XX.

Across his breast a crimson spot,

    That in a quiver glowed,

The ruddy crested camp-fires shot,

    As he to darkness rode.

XXI.

He rode while omens called, beware

    Old Kraken's pledge of faith !

A smile and waving hand in air,

    And outward flew the wraith.

XXII.

Before pale morn had mixed with gold,

    His army roared, and chilled,

As men who have a woe foretold,

    And see it red fulfilled.

XXIII.

Away and to his young wife speed,

    And say that Honour's dead!

Another word she will not need

    To bow a widow's head.

XXIV.

Old Kraken roped his white moustache

    Right, left, for savage glee:

—To swing him in his soldier's sash,

    Were kind for such as he!

XXV.

Old Kraken's look hard Winter wears

    When sweeps the wild snow-blast:

He had the hug of Arctic bears

    For captives he held fast.

II.

I.

ARCHDUCHESS ANNE sat carved in frost,
　　Shut off from priest and spouse.
Her lips were locked, her arms were crossed,
　　Her eyes were in her brows.

II.

One hand enclosed a paper scroll,
　　Held as a strangled asp.
So may we see the woman's soul
　　In her dire tempter's grasp.

III.

Along that scroll Count Louis' doom

Throbbed till the letters flamed.

She saw him in his scornful bloom,

She saw him chained and shamed.

IV.

Around that scroll Count Louis' fate

Was acted to her stare,

And hate in love and love in hate

Fought fell to smite or spare.

V.

Between the day that struck her old,

And this black star of days,

Her heart swung like a storm-bell tolled

Above a town ablaze.

VI.

His beauty pressed to intercede,

His beauty served him ill.

—Not Vengeance, 'tis his rebel's deed,

'Tis Justice, not our will!

VII.

Yet who had sprung to life's full force

A breast that loveless dried?

But who had sapped it at the source,

With scarlet to her pride!

VIII.

He brought her human wane as 'twere

New message from the skies.

And he betrayed, and left on her

The burden of their sighs.

IX.

In floods her tender memories poured;

They foamed with waves of spite:

She crushed them, high her heart outsoared,

To keep her mind alight.

X.

—The crawling creature, called in scorn

A woman!—with this pen

We sign a paper that may warn

His crowing fellowmen.

XI.

—We read them lesson of a power

They slight who do us wrong.

That bitter hour this bitter hour

Provokes ; by turns the strong !

XII.

—That we were woman once is known :

That we are Justice now,

Above our sex, above the throne,

Men quaking shall avow.

XIII.

Archduchess Anne ascending flew,

Her heart outsoared, but felt

The demon of her sex pursue,

Incensing or to melt.

XIV.

Those counterfloods below at leap,

Still in her breast blew storm,

And farther up the heavenly steep,

Wrestled in angels' form.

XV.

To disentangle one clear wish

Not of her sex, she sought ;

And womanish to womanish,

Discerned in lighted thought.

XVI.

With Louis' chance it went not well

When at herself she raged ;

A woman, of whom men might tell

She doted, crazed and aged.

XVII.

Or else enamoured of a sweet

Withdrawn, a vengeful crone !

And say, what figure at her feet

Is this that utters moan ?

XVIII.

The Countess Louis from her head

Drew veil : 'Great Lady, hear !

My husband deems you Justice dread,

I know you Mercy dear.

XIX.

'His error upon him may fall;

He will not breathe a nay.

I am his helpless mate in all,

Except for grace to pray.

XX.

'Perchance on me his choice inclined,

To give his House an heir:

I had not marriage with his mind,

His counsel could not share.

XXI.

'I brought no portion for his weal

But this one instinct true,

Which bids me in my weakness kneel,

Archduchess Anne, to you.'

XXII.

The frowning Lady uttered, 'Forth!'

Her look forbade delay.

'It is not mine to weigh your worth;

Your husband's others weigh.

XXIII.

'Hence with the woman in your speech,

For nothing it avails

In woman's fashion to beseech

Where Justice holds the scales.'

XXIV.

Then bent and went the lady wan,

Whose girlishness made grey

The thoughts that through Archduchess Anne

Shattered like stormy spray.

XXV.

Long sat she there, as flame that strives

To hold on beating wind :

—His wife must be the fool of wives,

Or cunningly designed !

XXVI.

She sat until the tempest-pitch

In her torn bosom fell ;

—His wife must be a subtle witch

Or else God loves her well !

III.

I.

OLD Kraken read a missive penned
  By his great Lady's hand.
Her condescension called him friend,
  To raise the crest she fanned.

II.

Swiftly to where he lay encamped
  It flew, yet breathed aloof
From woman's feeling, and he stamped
  A heel more like a hoof.

T   C

III.

She wrote of Mercy : 'She was loth

Too hard to goad a foe.'

He stamped, as when men drive an oath

Devils transcribe below.

IV.

She wrote : 'We have him half by theft.'

His wrinkles glistened keen :

And see the Winter storm-cloud cleft

To lurid skies between !

V.

When read old Kraken : 'Christ our Guide,'

His eyes were spikes of spar :

And see the white snow-storm divide

About an icy star !

VI.

'She trusted him to understand,'

She wrote, and further prayed

That policy might rule the land.

Old Kraken's laughter neighed.

VII.

Her words he took; her nods and winks

Treated as woman's fog.

The man-dog for his mistress thinks,

Not less her faithful dog.

VIII.

She hugged a cloak old Kraken ripped;

Disguise to him he loathed.

—Your mercy, madam, shows you stripped,

While mine will keep you clothed.

IX.

A rough ill-soldered scar in haste

He rubbed on his cheek-bone.

—Our policy the man shall taste;

Our mercy shall be shown.

X.

'Count Louis, honour to your race

Decrees the Council-hall:

You 'scape the rope by special grace,

And like a soldier fall.'

XI.

—I am a man of many sins,

Who for one virtue die,

Count Louis said.—They play at shins,

Who kick, was the reply.

XII.

Uprose the day of crimson sight,

The day without a God.

At morn the hero said Good-night :

See there that stain on sod !

XIII.

At morn the Countess Louis heard

Young light sing in the lark.

Ere eve it was that other bird,

Which brings the starless dark.

XIV.

To heaven she vowed herself, and yearned

Beside her lord to lie.

Archduchess Anne on Kraken turned,

All white as a dead eye.

XV.

If I could kill thee ! shrieked her look :

If lightning sprang from Will !

An oaken head old Kraken shook,

And she might thank or kill.

XVI.

The pride that fenced her heart in mail,

By mortal pain was torn.

Forth from her bosom leaped a wail,

As of a babe new-born.

XVII.

She clad herself in courtly use,

And one who heard them prate,

Had said they differed upon views

Where statecraft raised debate.

XVIII.

The wretch detested must she trust,

The servant master own :

Confide to godless cause so just,

And for God's blessing moan.

XIX.

Austerely she her heart kept down,

Her woman's tongue was mute

When voice of People, voice of Crown,

In cannon held dispute.

XX.

The Crown on seas of blood, like swine,

Swam forefoot at the throat :

It drank of its dear veins for wine,

Enough if it might float !

XXI.

It sank with piteous yelp, resurged

Electrical with fear.

O had she on old Kraken urged

Her word of mercy clear !

XXII.

O had they with Count Louis been

Accordant in his plea !

Cursed are the women vowed to screen

A heart that all can see !

XXIII.

The godless drove unto a goal

Was worse than vile defeat.

Did vengeance prick Count Louis' soul

They dressed him luscious meat.

XXIV.

Worms will the faithless find their lies

In the close treasure-chest.

Without a God no day can rise,

Though it should slay our best.

XXV.

The Crown it furled a draggled flag,

It sheathed a broken blade.

Behold its triumph in the hag

That lives with looks decayed !

XXVI.

And lo, the man of oaken head,

Of soldier's honour bare,

He fled his land, but most he fled

His Lady's frigid stare.

XXVII.

Judged by the issue we discern

God's blessing, and the bane.

Count Louis' dust would fill an urn,

His deeds are waving grain.

XXVIII.

And she that helped to slay, yet bade

To spare the fated man,

Great were her errors, but she had

Great heart, Archduchess Anne.

THE SONG OF THEODOLINDA

I.

QUEEN THEODOLIND has built
In the earth a furnace-bed :
There the Traitor Nail that spilt
Blood of the anointed Head,
Red of heat, resolves in shame :
White of heat, awakes to flame.

> Beat, beat ! white of heat,
> Red of heat, beat, beat !

II.

Mark the skeleton of fire

Lightening from its thunder-roof :

So comes this that saw expire

Him we love, for our behoof !

Red of heat, O white of heat,

This from off the Cross we greet.

III.

Brown-cowled hammermen around

Nerve their naked arms to strike

Death with Resurrection crowned,

Each upon that cruel spike.

Red of heat the furnace leaps,

White of heat transfigured sleeps.

IV.

Hard against the furnace core

Holds the Queen her streaming eyes :

Lo ! that thing of piteous gore

In the lap of radiance lies,

Red of heat, as when He takes,

White of heat, whom earth forsakes.

V.

Forth with it, and crushing ring

Iron hymns, for men to hear

Echoes of the deeds that sting

Earth into its graves, and fear !

Red of heat, He maketh thus,

White of heat, a crown of us.

VI.

This that killed Thee, kissed Thee, Lord !

Touched Thee, and we touch it : dear,

Dark it is ; adored, abhorred :

Vilest, yet most sainted here.

Red of heat, O white of heat,

In it hell and heaven meet.

VII.

I behold our morning day

When they chased Him out with rods

Up to where this traitor lay

Thirsting; and the blood was God's !

Red of heat, it shall be pressed,

White of heat, once on my breast !

VIII.

Quick ! the reptile in me shrieks,

Not the soul.   Again ; the Cross

Burn there.   Oh ! this pain it wreaks

Rapture is : pain is not loss.

Red of heat, the tooth of Death,

White of heat, has caught my breath.

IX.

Brand me, bite me, bitter thing !

Thus He felt, and thus I am

One with Him in suffering,

One with Him in bliss, the Lamb.

Red of heat, O white of heat,

Thus is bitterness made sweet.

X.

Now am I, who bear that stamp

Scorched in me, the living sign

Sole on earth—the lighted lamp

Of the dreadful day divine.

White of heat, beat on it fast!

Red of heat, its shape has passed.

XI.

Out in angry sparks they fly,

They that sentenced Him to bleed :

Pontius and his troop : they die,

Damned for ever for the deed!

White of heat in vain they soar :

Red of heat they strew the floor.

XII.

Fury on it ! have its debt !

Thunder on the Hill accurst,

Golgotha, be ye ! and sweat

Blood, and thirst the Passion's thirst.

Red of heat and white of heat,

Champ it like fierce teeth that eat.

XIII.

Strike it as the ages crush

Towers ! for while a shape is seen

I am rivalled. Quench its blush,

Devil ! But it crowns me Queen,

Red of heat, as none before,

White of heat, the circlet wore.

XIV.

Lowly I will be, and quail,

Crawling, with a beggar's hand :

On my breast the branded Nail,

On my head the iron band.

Red of heat, are none so base!

White of heat, none know such grace!

xv.

In their heaven the sainted hosts,

Robed in violet unflecked,

Gaze on humankind as ghosts :

I draw down a ray direct.

Red of heat, across my brow,

White of heat, I touch Him now.

xvi.

Robed in violet, robed in gold,

Robed in pearl, they make our dawn.

What am I to them ?   Behold

What ye are to me, and fawn.

Red of heat, be humble, ye !

White of heat, O teach it me !

XVII.

Martyrs ! hungry peaks in air,

Rent with lightnings, clad with snow,

Crowned with stars ! you strip me bare,

Pierce me, shame me, stretch me low,

Red of heat, but it may be,

White of heat, some envy me !

XVIII.

O poor enviers !   God's own gifts

Have a devil for the weak.

Yea, the very force that lifts

Finds the vessel's secret leak.

Red of heat, I rise o'er all :

White of heat, I faint, I fall.

XIX.

Those old Martyrs sloughed their pride,

Taking humbleness like mirth.

I am to His Glory tied,

I that witness Him on earth !

Red of heat, my pride of dust,

White of heat, feeds fire in trust.

XX.

Kindle me to constant fire,

Lest the nail be but a nail !

Give me wings of great desire,

Lest I look within, and fail !

Red of heat, the furnace light,

White of heat, fix on my sight.

XXI.

Never for the Chosen peace !

Know, by me tormented know,

Never shall the wrestling cease

Till with our outlasting Foe,

Red of heat to white of heat,

Roll we to the Godhead's feet !

Beat, beat ! white of heat,

Red of heat, beat, beat !

XXII.

Red of heat the firebrands die.

White of heat the ashes lie.

A PREACHING FROM A SPANISH BALLAD

I.

LADIES who in chains of wedlock
Chafe at an unequal yoke,
Not to nightingales give hearing;
Better this, the raven's croak.

II.

Down the Prado strolled my seigneur,
Arm at lordly bow on hip,
Fingers trimming his moustachios,
Eyes for pirate fellowship.

III.

Home sat she that owned him master;

Like the flower bent to ground

Rain-surcharged and sun-forsaken;

Heedless of her hair unbound.

IV.

Sudden at her feet a lover

Palpitating knelt and wooed;

Seemed a very gift from heaven

To the starved of common food.

V.

Love me? she his vows repeated:

Fiery vows oft sung and thrummed:

Wondered, as on earth a stranger;

Thirsted, trusted, and succumbed.

VI.

O beloved youth! my lover!

Mine! my lover! take my life

Wholly: thine in soul and body,

By this oath of more than wife!

VII.

Know me for no helpless woman ;

Nay, nor coward, though I sink

Awed beside thee, like an infant

Learning shame ere it can think.

VIII.

Swing me hence to do thee service,

Be thy succour, prove thy shield ;

Heaven will hear !—in house thy handmaid,

Squire upon the battlefield.

IX.

At my breasts I cool thy footsoles ;

Wine I pour, I dress thy meats ;

Humbly, when my lord it pleaseth,

Lie with him on perfumed sheets :

X.

Pray for him, my blood's dear fountain,

While he sleeps, and watch his yawn

In that wakening babelike moment,

Sweeter to my thought than dawn !—

XI.

Thundered then her lord of thunders ;

Burst the door, and flashing sword,

Loud disgorged the woman's title :

Condemnation in one word.

XII.

Grand by righteous wrath transfigured,

Towers the husband who provides '

In his person judge and witness,

Death's black doorkeeper besides !

XIII.

Round his head the ancient terrors,

Conjured of the stronger's law,

Circle, to abash the creature

Daring twist beneath his paw.

XIV.

How though he hath squandered Honour !

High of Honour let him scold :

Gilding of the man's possession,

'Tis the woman's coin of gold.

XV.

She inheriting from many

Bleeding mothers bleeding sense,

Feels 'twixt her and sharp-fanged nature

Honour first did plant the fence.

XVI.

Nature, that so shrieks for justice ;

Honour's thirst, that blood will slake ;

These are women's riddles, roughly

Mixed to write them saint or snake.

XVII.

Never nature cherished woman :

She throughout the sexes' war

Serves as temptress and betrayer,

Favouring man, the muscular.

XVIII.

Lureful is she, bent for folly ;

Doating on the child which crows :

Yours to teach him grace in fealty,

What the bloom is, what the rose.

XIX.

Hard the task : your prison-chamber

Widens not for lifted latch

Till the giant thews and sinews

Meet their Godlike overmatch.

XX.

Read that riddle, scorning pity's

Tears, of cockatrices shed :

When the heart is vowed for freedom,

Captaincy it yields to head.

XXI.

Meanwhile you, freaked nature's martyrs,

Honour's army, flower and weed,

Gentle ladies, wedded ladies,

See for you this fair one bleed.

XXII.

Sole stood her offence, she faltered ;

Prayed her lord the youth to spare ;

Prayed that in the orange garden

She might lie, and ceased her prayer.

XXIII.

Then commending to all women

Chastity, her breasts she laid

Bare unto the self-avenger.

Man in metal was the blade.

THE YOUNG PRINCESS

A BALLAD OF OLD LAWS OF LOVE

I.

I.

WHEN the South sang like a nightingale
    Above a bower in May,
The training of Love's vine of flame
Was writ in laws, for lord and dame
    To say their yea and nay.

II.

When the South sang like a nightingale

Across the flowering night,

And lord and dame held gentle sport,

There came a young princess to Court,

A frost of beauty white.

III.

The South sang like a nightingale

To thaw her glittering dream :

No vine of Love her bosom gave,

She drank no wine of Love, but grave

She held them to Love's theme.

IV.

The South grew all a nightingale

Beneath a moon unmoved :

Like the banner of war she led them on ;

She left them to lie, like the light that has gone

From wine-cups overproved.

V.

When the South was a fervid nightingale,

And she a chilling moon,

'Twas pity to see on the garden swards,

Against Love's laws, those rival lords

As willow-wands lie strewn.

VI.

The South had throat of a nightingale

For her, the young princess :

She gave no vine of Love to rear,

Love's wine drank not, yet bent her ear

To themes of Love no less.

II

I.

THE lords of the Court they sighed heart-sick,

    Heart-free Lord Dusiote laughed :

I prize her no more than a fling o' the dice,

But, or shame to my manhood, a lady of ice,

    We master her by craft !

II.

Heart-sick the lords of joyance yawned,

    Lord Dusiote laughed heart-free :

I count her as much as a crack o' my thumb,

But, or shame of my manhood, to me she shall come

    Like the bird to roost in the tree !

III.

At dead of night when the palace-guard

　　Had passed the measured rounds,

The young princess awoke to feel

A shudder of blood at the crackle of steel

　　Within the garden-bounds.

IV.

It ceased, and she thought of whom was need,

　　The friar or the leech ;

When lo, stood her tirewoman breathless by :

Lord Dusiote, madam, to death is nigh,

　　Of you he would have speech.

V.

He prays you of your gentleness,

　　To light him to his dark end.

The princess rose, and forth she went,

For charity was her intent,

　　Devoutly to befriend.

VI.

Lord Dusiote hung on his good squire's arm,

    The priest beside him knelt :

A weeping handkerchief was pressed

To stay the red flood at his breast,

    And bid cold ladies melt.

VII.

O lady, though you are ice to men,

    All pure to heaven as light

Within the dew within the flower,

Of you 'tis whispered that love has power

    When secret is the night.

VIII.

I have silenced the slanderers, peace to their souls !

    Save one was too cunning for me.

I die, whose love is late avowed,

He lives, who boasts the lily has bowed

    To the oath of a bended knee.

IX.

Lord Dusiote drew breath with pain,

And she with pain drew breath :

On him she looked, on his like above ;

She flew in the folds of a marvel of love,

Revealed to pass to death.

X.

You are dying, O great-hearted lord,

You are dying for me, she cried ;

O take my hand, O take my kiss,

And take of your right for love like this,

The vow that plights me bride.

XI.

She bade the priest recite his words

While hand in hand were they,

Lord Dusiote's soul to waft to bliss ;

He had her hand, her vow, her kiss,

And his body was borne away.

III

I

LORD DUSIOTE sprang from priest and squire ;

    He gazed at her lighted room :

The laughter in his heart grew slack ;

He knew not the force that pushed him back

    From her and the morn in bloom.

II.

Like a drowned man's length on the strong flood-tide,

    Like the shade of a bird in the sun,

He fled from his lady whom he might claim

As ghost, and who made the daybeams flame

    To scare what he had done.

T   E

III.

There was grief at Court for one so gay,

Though he was a lord less keen

For training the vine than at vintage-press ;

But in her soul the young princess

Believed that love had been.

IV.

Lord Dusiote fled the Court and land,

He crossed the woeful seas,

Till his traitorous doing seemed clearer to burn,

And the lady beloved drew his heart for return,

Like the banner of war in the breeze.

V

He neared the palace, he spied the Court,

And music he heard, and they told

Of foreign lords arrived to bring

The nuptial gifts of a bridegroom king

To the princess grave and cold.

VI.

The masque and the dance were cloud on wave,

And down the masque and the dance

Lord Dusiote stepped from dame to dame,

And to the young princess he came,

With a bow and a burning glance.

VII.

Do you take a new husband to-morrow, lady ?

She shrank as at prick of steel.

Must the first yield place to the second, he sighed.

Her eyes were like the grave that is wide

For the corpse from head to heel.

VIII.

My lady, my love, that little hand

Has mine ringed fast in plight :

I bear for your lips a lawful thirst,

And as justly the second should follow the first,

I come to your door this night.

IX.

If a ghost should come a ghost will go :

No more the lady said,

Save that ever when he in wrath began

To swear by the faith of a living man,

She answered him, You are dead.

IV.

I.

THE soft night-wind went laden to death
    With smell of the orange in flower ;
The light leaves prattled to neighbour ears ;
The bird of the passion sang over his tears ;
    The night named hour by hour.

II.

Sang loud, sang low the rapturous bird
    Till the yellow hour was nigh,
Behind the folds of a darker cloud :
He chuckled, he sobbed, alow, aloud ;
    The voice between earth and sky.

III.

O will you, will you, women are weak ;

The proudest are yielding mates

For a forward foot and a tongue of fire :

So thought Lord Dusiote's trusty squire,

At watch by the palace-gates.

IV.

The song of the bird was wine in his blood,

And woman the odorous bloom :

His master's great adventure stirred

Within him to mingle the bloom and bird,

And morn ere its coming illume.

V.

Beside him strangely a piece of the dark

Had moved, and the undertones

Of a priest in prayer, like a cavernous wave,

He heard, as were there a soul to save

For urgency now in the groans.

VI

No priest was hired for the play this night :

And the squire tossed head like a deer

At sniff of the tainted wind ; he gazed

Where cresset-lamps in a door were raised,

Belike on a passing bier.

VII.

All cloaked and masked, with naked blades,

That flashed of a judgement done,

The lords of the Court, from the palace-door,

Came issuing silently, bearers four,

And flat on their shoulders one.

VIII.

They marched the body to squire and priest,

They lowered it sad to earth :

The priest they gave the burial dole,

Bade wrestle hourly for his soul,

Who was a lord of worth.

IX.

One said, farewell to a gallant knight !

And one, but a restless ghost !

'Tis a year and a day since in this place

He died, sped high by a lady of grace

To join the blissful host.

X.

Not vainly on us she charged her cause,

The lady whom we revere

For faith in the mask of a love untrue

To the Love we honour, the Love her due,

The Love we have vowed to rear.

XI.

A trap for the sweet tooth, lures for the light,

For the fortress defiant a mine :

Right well !   But not in the South, princess,

Shall the lady snared of her nobleness

Ever shamed or a captive pine.

XII.

When the South had voice of a nightingale

　　Above a Maying bower,

On the heights of Love walked radiant peers ;

The bird of the passion sang over his tears

　　To the breeze and the orange-flower.

KING HARALD'S TRANCE

I.

SWORD in length a reaping-hook amain
Harald sheared his field, blood up to shank :
'Mid the swathes of slain,
First at moonrise drank.

II.

Thereof hunger, as for meats the knife,
Pricked his ribs, in one sharp spur to reach
Home and his young wife,
Nigh the sea-ford beach.

III.

After battle keen to feed was he :

Smoking flesh the thresher washed down fast,

Like an angry sea

Ships from keel to mast.

IV.

Name us glory, singer, name us pride

Matching Harald's in his deeds of strength ;

Chiefs, wife, sword by side,

Foemen stretched their length !

V.

Half a winter night the toasts hurrahed,

Crowned him, clothed him, trumpeted him high,

Till awink he bade

Wife to chamber fly.

VI.

Twice the sun had mounted, twice had sunk,

Ere his ears took sound ; he lay for dead ;

Mountain on his trunk,

Ocean on his head.

VII.

Clamped to couch, his fiery hearing sucked

Whispers that at heart made iron-clang :

Here fool-women clucked,

There men held harangue.

VIII.

Burial to fit their lord of war,

They decreed him : hailed the kingling : ha !

Hateful ! but this Thor

Failed a weak lamb's baa.

IX.

King they hailed a branchlet, shaped to fare,

Weighted so, like quaking shingle spume,

When his blood's own heir

Ripened in the womb !

X.

Still he heard, and doglike, hoglike, ran

Nose of hearing till his blind sight saw :

Woman stood with man

Mouthing low, at paw.

XI.

Woman, man, they mouthed; they spake a thing

Armed to split a mountain, sunder seas :

Still the frozen king

Lay and felt him freeze.

XII.

Doglike, hoglike, horselike now he raced,

Riderless, in ghost across a ground

Flint of breast, blank-faced,

Past the fleshly bound.

XIII.

Smell of brine his nostrils filled with might :

Nostrils quickened eyelids, eyelids hand :

Hand for sword at right

Groped, the great haft spanned.

XIV.

Wonder struck to ice his people's eyes :

Him they saw, the prone upon the bier,

Sheer from backbone rise,

Sword uplifting peer.

XV.

Sitting did he breathe against the blade,

Standing kiss it for that proof of life :

Strode, as netters wade,

Straightway to his wife.

XVI.

Her he eyed : his judgement was one word,

Foulbed ! and she fell : the blow clove two.

Fearful for the third,

All their breath indrew.

XVII.

Morning danced along the waves to beach ;

Dumb his chiefs fetched breath for what might hap :

Glassily on each

Stared the iron cap.

XVIII.

Sudden, as it were a monster oak

Split to yield a limb by stress of heat,

Strained he, staggered, broke

Doubled at their feet.

WHIMPER OF SYMPATHY

HAWK or shrike has done this deed
Of downy feathers : rueful sight !
Sweet sentimentalist, invite
Your bosom's Power to intercede.

So hard it seems that one must bleed
Because another needs will bite !
All round we find cold Nature slight
The feelings of the totter-knee'd.

O it were pleasant, with you

To fly from this tussle of foes,

The shambles, the charnel, the wrinkle !

To dwell in yon dribble of dew

On the cheek of your sovereign rose,

And live the young life of a twinkle.

YOUNG REYNARD

I.

GRACEFULLEST leaper, the dappled fox-cub
Curves over brambles with berries and buds,
Light as a bubble that flies from the tub,
Whisked by the laundry-wife out of her suds.
Wavy he comes, woolly, all at his ease,
Elegant, fashioned to foot with the deuce;
Nature's own prince of the dance: then he sees
Me, and retires as if making excuse.

T   F

II.

Never closed minuet courtlier !	Soon

Cub-hunting troops were abroad, and a yelp

Told of sure scent : ere the stroke upon noon

Reynard the younger lay far beyond help.

Wild, my poor friend, has the fate to be chased ;

Civil will conquer : were 'tother 'twere worse,

Fair, by the flushed early morning embraced,

Haply you live a day longer in verse.

MANFRED

I.

PROJECTED from the bilious Childe,

This clatterjaw his foot could set

On Alps, without a breast beguiled

To glow in shedding rascal sweat.

Somewhere about his grinder teeth,

He mouthed of thoughts that grilled beneath,

And summoned Nature to her feud

With bile & buskin Attitude.

II.

Considerably was the world

Of spinsterdom and clergy racked

While he his hinted horrors hurled,

And she pictorially attacked.

A duel hugeous! Tragic? Ho!

The cities, not the mountains, blow

Such bladders ; in their shapes confessed

An after-dinner's indigest.

HERNANI

CISTERCIANS might crack their sides

With laughter, and exemption get,

At sight of heroes clasping brides,

And hearing—O the horn ! the horn !

The horn of their obstructive debt !

But quit the stage, that note applies

For sermons cosmopolitan,

Hernani.   Have we filched our prize,

Forgetting .   .?   O the horn ! the horn !

The horn of the Old Gentleman !

THE NUPTIALS OF ATTILA

I.

FLAT as to an eagle's eye,

    Earth hung under Attila.

Sign for carnage gave he none.

In the peace of his disdain,

Sun and rain, and rain and sun,

Cherished men to wax again,

Crawl, and in their manner die.

On his people stood a frost.

Like the charger cut in stone,

Rearing stiff, the warrior host,

Which had life from him alone,

Craved the trumpet's eager note,

As the bridled earth the Spring.

Rusty was the trumpet's throat.

He let chief and prophet rave ;

Venturous earth around him string

Threads of grass and slender rye,

Wave them, and untrampled wave.

O for the time when God did cry,

 Eye and have, my Attila !

II.

Scorn of conquest filled like sleep

Him that drank of havoc deep

When the Green Cat pawed the globe :

When the horsemen from his bow

Shot in sheaves and made the foe

Crimson fringes of a robe,

Trailed o'er towns and fields in woe ;

When they streaked the rivers red,

When the saddle was the bed.

Attila, my Attila !

III.

He breathed peace and pulled a flower.

Eye and have, my Attila !

This was the damsel Ildico,

Rich in bloom until that hour :

Shyer than the forest doe

Twinkling slim through branches green.

Yet the shyest shall be seen.

Make the bed for Attila !

IV.

Seen of Attila, desired,

She was led to him straightway :

Radiantly was she attired ;

Rifled lands were her array,

Jewels bled from weeping crowns,

Gold of woeful fields and towns.

She stood pallid in the light.

How she walked, how withered white,

From the blessing to the board,

She who should have proudly blushed

Women whispered, asking why,

Hinting of a youth, and hushed.

Was it terror of her lord?

Was she childish? was she sly?

Was it the bright mantle's dye

Drained her blood to hues of grief

Like the ash that shoots the spark?

See the green tree all in leaf:

See the green tree stripped of bark!—

Make the bed for Attila!

V.

Round the banquet-table's load
Scores of iron horsemen rode ;
Chosen warriors, keen and hard ;
Grain of threshing battle-dints ;
Attila's fierce body-guard,
Smelling war like fire in flints.
Grant them peace be fugitive !
Iron-capped and iron-heeled,
Each against his fellow's shield
Smote the spear-head, shouting, Live,
　　Attila ! my Attila !
Eagle, eagle of our breed,
Eagle, beak the lamb, and feed !
Have her, and unleash us ! live,
　　Attila ! my Attila !

VI.

He was of the blood to shine
Bronze in joy, like skies that scorch.

Beaming with the goblet wine

In the wavering of the torch,

Looked he backward on his bride.

Eye and have, my Attila !

Fair in her wide robe was she :

Where the robe and vest divide,

Fair she seemed surpassingly :

Soft, yet vivid as the stream

Danube rolls in the moonbeam

Through rock-barriers : but she smiled

Never, she sat cold as salt :

Open-mouthed as a young child

Wondering with a mind at fault.

Make the bed for Attila !

VII.

Under the thin hoop of gold

Whence in waves her hair outrolled,

'Twixt her brows the women saw

Shadows of a vulture's claw

Gript in flight: strange knots that sped

Closing and dissolving aye:

Such as wicked dreams betray

When pale dawn creeps o'er the bed.

They might show the common pang

Known to virgins, in whom dread

Hunts their bliss like famished hounds;

While the chiefs with roaring rounds

Tossed her to her lord, and sang

Praise of him whose hand was large,

Cheers for beauty brought to yield,

Chirrups of the trot afield,

Hurrahs of the battle-charge.

VIII.

Those rock-faces hung with weed

Reddened: their great days of speed,

Slaughter, triumph, flood and flame,

Like a jealous frenzy wrought,

Scoffed at them and did them shame,

Quaffing idle, conquering naught.

O for the time when God decreed

    Earth the prey of Attila !

God called on thee in his wrath,

Trample it to mire !   'Twas done.

Swift as Danube clove our path

Down from East to Western sun.

Huns ! behold your pasture, gaze,

Take, our king said : heel to flank

(Whisper it, the warhorse neighs !)

Forth we drove, and blood we drank

Fresh as dawn-dew : earth was ours :

Men were flocks we lashed and spurned :

Fast as windy flame devours,

Flame along the wind, we burned.

Arrow, javelin, spear, and sword !

Here the snows and there the plains ;

On ! our signal : onward poured

Torrents of the tightened reins,

Foaming over vine and corn

Hot against the city-wall.

Whisper it, you sound a horn

To the grey beast in the stall !

Yea, he whinnies at a nod.

O for sound of the trumpet-notes !

O for the time when thunder-shod,

He that scarce can munch his oats,

Hung on the peaks, brooded aloof,

Champed the grain of the wrath of God,

Pressed a cloud on the cowering roof,

Snorted out of the blackness fire !

Scarlet broke the sky, and down,

Hammering West with print of his hoof,

He burst out of the bosom of ire

Sharp as eyelight under thy frown,

  Attila, my Attila !

IX.

Ravaged cities rolling smoke

Thick on cornfields dry and black,

Wave his banners, bear his yoke.

Track the lightning, and you track

Attila.   They moan : 'tis he !

Bleed : 'tis he !   Beneath his foot

Leagues are deserts charred and mute ;

Where he passed, there passed a sea.

        Attila, my Attila !

X.

—Who breathed on the king cold breath ?

Said a voice amid the host,

He is Death that weds a ghost,

Else a ghost that weds with Death ?

Ildico's chill little hand

Shuddering he beheld : austere

Stared, as one who would command

Sight of what has filled his ear :

Plucked his thin beard, laughed disdain.

Feast, ye Huns! His arm he raised,

Like the warrior, battle-dazed,

Joining to the fight amain.

    Make the bed for Attila !

XI.

Silent Ildico stood up.

King and chief to pledge her well,

Shocked sword sword and cup on cup

Clamouring like a brazen bell.

Silent stepped the queenly slave.

Fair, by heaven ! she was to meet

On a midnight, near a grave,

Flapping wide the winding-sheet.

XII.

Death and she walked through the crowd,

Out beyond the flush of light.

Ceremonious women bowed

Following her : 'twas middle night.

Then the warriors each on each   ˙

Spied, nor overloudly laughed ;

Like the victims of the leech,

Who have drunk of a strange draught.

XIII.

Attila remained.   Even so

Frowned he when he struck the blow,

Brained his horse that stumbled twice,

On a bloody day in Gaul,

Bellowing, Perish omens !   All

Marvelled at the sacrifice,

But the battle, swinging dim,   ˌ

Rang off that axe-blow for him.

   Attila, my Attila !

T   G   .

XIV.

Brightening over Danube wheeled

Star by star ; and she, most fair,

• Sweet as victory half-revealed,

Seized to make him glad and young ;

She, O sweet as the dark sign

Given him oft in battles gone,

When the voice within said, Dare !

And the trumpet-notes were sprung

Rapturous for the charge in line :

She lay waiting : fair as dawn

Wrapped in folds of night she lay ;

Secret, lustrous ; flaglike there,

Waiting him to stream and ray,

With one loosening blush outflung,

Colours of his hordes of horse

Ranked for combat : still he hung

, Like the fever dreading air,

Cursed of heat ; and as a corse

Gathers vultures, in his brain

Images of her eyes and kiss

Plucked at the limbs that could remain

Loitering nigh the doors of bliss.

Make the bed for Attila !

XV.

Passion on one hand, on one,

Destiny led forth the Hun.

Heard ye outcries of affright,

Voices that through many a fray,

In the press of flag and spear,

Warned the king of peril near ?

Men were dumb, they gave him way,

Eager heads to left and right,

Like the bearded standard, thrust,

As in battle, for a nod

From their lord of battle-dust.

Attila, my Attila !

Slow between the lines he trod.

Saw ye not the sun drop slow

On this nuptial day, ere eve

Pierced him on the couch aglow ?

　　　Attila, my Attila !

Here and there his heart would cleave

Clotted memory for a space :

Some stout chief's familiar face,

Choicest of his fighting brood,

Touched him, as 'twere one to know

Ere he met his bride's embrace.

　　　Attila, my Attila !

Twisting fingers in a beard

Scant as winter underwood,

With a narrowed eye he peered ;

Like the sunset's graver red

Up old pine-stems.   Grave he stood

Eyeing them on whom was shed

Burning light from him alone.

　　　Attila, my Attila !

Red were they whose mouths recalled

Where the slaughter mounted high,

High on it, o'er earth appalled,

He ; heaven's finger in their sight

Raising him on waves of dead :

Up to heaven his trumpets blown.

O for the time when God's delight

    Crowned the head of Attila !

Hungry river of the crag

Stretching hands for earth he came :

Force and Speed astride his name

Pointed back to spear and flag.

He came out of miracle cloud,

Lightning-swift and spectre-lean.

Now those days are in a shroud :

Have him to his ghostly queen.

    Make the bed for Attila !

XVI.

One, with winecups overstrung,

Cried him farewell in Rome's tongue.

Who ? for the great king turned as though

Wrath to the shaft's head strained the bow.

Nay, not wrath the king possessed,

But a radiance of the breast.

In that sound he had the key

Of his cunning malady.

Lo, where gleamed the sapphire lake,

Leo, with his Rome at stake,

Drew blank air to hues and forms ;

Whereof Two that shone distinct,

Linked as orbed stars are linked,

Clear among the myriad swarms,

In a constellation, dashed

Full on horse and rider's eyes

Sunless light, but light it was—

Light that blinded and abashed,

Froze his members, bade him pause,

Caught him mid-gallop, blazed him home.

　　　Attila, my Attila !

What are streams that cease to flow ?

What was Attila, rolled thence,

Cheated by a juggler's show?

Like that lake of blue intense,

Under tempest lashed to foam,

Lurid radiance, as he passed,

Filled him, and around was glassed,

When deep-voiced he uttered, Rome!

XVII.

Rome! the word was: and like meat

Flung to dogs the word was torn.

Soon Rome's magic priests shall bleat

Round their magic Pope forlorn!

Loud they swore the king had sworn

Vengeance on the Roman cheat,

Ere he passed as, grave and still,

Danube through the shouting hill:

Sworn it by his naked life!

Eagle, snakes these women are :

Take them on the wing ! but war,

Smoking war's the warrior's wife !

Then for plunder ! then for brides

Won without a winking priest !—

Danube whirled his train of tides

Black toward the yellow East.

    Make the bed for Attila !

XVIII.

Chirrups of the trot afield,

Hurrahs of the battle-charge,

How they answered, how they pealed,

When the morning rose and drew

Bow and javelin, lance and targe,

In the nuptial casement's view !

    Attila, my Attila !

Down the hillspurs, out of tents

Glimmering in mid-forest, through

Mists of the cool morning scents,

Forth from city-alley, court,

Arch, the bounding horsemen flew,

Joined along the plains of dew,

Raced and gave the rein to sport,

Closed and streamed like curtain-rents

Fluttered by a wind, and flowed

Into squadrons : trumpets blew,

Chargers neighed, and trappings glowed

Brave as the bright Orient's.

Look on the seas that run to greet

Sunrise : look on the leagues of wheat :

Look on the lines and squares that fret

Leaping to level the lance blood-wet.

Tens of thousands, man and steed,

Tossing like field-flowers in Spring ;

Ready to be hurled at need

Whither their great lord may sling.

Finger Romeward, Romeward, King !

Attila, my Attila !

Still the woman holds him fast

As a night-flag round the mast.

XIX.

Nigh upon the fiery noon,

Out of ranks a roaring burst.

'Ware white women like the moon !

They are poison : they have thirst

First for love, and next for rule.

Jealous of the army, she ?

Ho, the little wanton fool !

We were his before she squealed

Blind for mother's milk, and heeled

Kicking on her mother's knee.

His in life and death are we :

She but one flower of a field.

We have given him bliss tenfold

In an hour to match her night :

    Attila, my Attila !

Still her arms the master hold,

As on wounds the scarf winds tight.

XX.

Over Danube day no more,

Like the warrior's planted spear,

Stood to hail the King : in fear

Western day knocked at his door.

    Attila, my Attila !

Sudden in the army's eyes

Rolled a blast of lights and cries :

Flashing through them : Dead are ye !

Dead, ye Huns, and torn piecemeal !

See the ordered army reel

Stricken through the ribs : and see,

Wild for speed to cheat despair,

Horsemen, clutching knee to chin,

Crouch and dart they know not where.

    Attila, my Attila !

Faces covered, faces bare,

Light the palace-front like jets

Of a dreadful fire within.

Beating hands and driving hair

Start on roof and parapets.

Dust rolls up ; the slaughter din.

—Death to them who call him dead !

Death to them who doubt the tale !

Choking in his dusty veil,

Sank the sun on his death-bed.

    Make the bed for Attila !

XXI.

'Tis the room where thunder sleeps.

Frenzy, as a wave to shore

Surging, burst the silent door,

And drew back to awful deeps,

Breath beaten out, foam-white.   Anew

Howled and pressed the ghastly crew,

Like storm-waters over rocks.

    Attila, my Attila !

One long shaft of sunset red

Laid a finger on the bed.

Horror, with the snaky locks,

Shocked the surge to stiffened heaps,

Hoary as the glacier's head

Faced to the moon.   Insane they look.

God it is in heaven who weeps

Fallen from his hand the Scourge he shook.

Make the bed for Attila !

XXII.

Square along the couch, and stark,

Like the sea-rejected thing

Sea-sucked white, behold their King.

Attila, my Attila !

Beams that panted black and bright,

Scornful lightnings danced their sight :

Him they see an oak in bud,

Him an oaklog stripped of bark :

Him, their lord of day and night,

White, and lifting up his blood

Dumb for vengeance.   Name us that,

Huddled in the corner dark,

Humped and grinning like a cat,

Teeth for lips !—'tis she ! she stares,

Glittering through her bristled hairs.

Rend her !   Pierce her to the hilt !

She is Murder : have her out !

What ! this little fist, as big

As the southern summer fig !

She is Madness, none may doubt.

Death, who dares deny her guilt !

Death, who says his blood she spilt !

Make the bed for Attila !

XXIII.

Torch and lamp and sunset-red

Fell three-fingered on the bed.

In the torch the beard-hair scant

With the great breast seemed to pant :

In the yellow lamp the limbs

Wavered, as the lake-flower swims :

In the sunset red the dead

Dead avowed him, dry blood-red.

XXIV.

Hatred of that abject slave,

Earth, was in each chieftain's heart.

Earth has got him, whom God gave,

Earth may sing, and earth shall smart !

    Attila, my Attila !

XXV.

Thus their prayer was raved and ceased.

Then had Vengeance of her feast

Scent in their quick pang to smite

Which they knew not, but huge pain

Urged them for some victim slain

Swift, and blotted from the sight.

Each at each, a crouching beast,

Glared, and quivered for the word.

Each at each, and all on that,

Humped and grinning like a cat,

Head-bound with its bridal-wreath.

Then the bitter chamber heard

Vengeance in a cauldron seethe.

Hurried counsel rage and craft

Yelped to hungry men, whose teeth

Hard the grey lip-ringlet gnawed,

Gleaming till their fury laughed.

With the steel-hilt in the clutch,

Eyes were shot on her that froze

In their blood-thirst overawed ;

Burned to rend, yet feared to touch.

She that was his nuptial rose,

She was of his heart's blood clad :

Oh ! the last of him she had !—

Could a little fist as big

As the southern summer fig,

Push a dagger's point to pierce

Ribs like those? Who else! They glared

Each at each. Suspicion fierce

Many a black remembrance bared.

Attila, my Attila!

Death, who dares deny her guilt!

Death, who says his blood she spilt!

Traitor he, who stands between!

Swift to hell, who harms the Queen!

She, the wild contention's cause,

Combed her hair with quiet paws.

Make the bed for Attila!

XXVI.

Night was on the host in arms.

Night, as never night before,

Hearkened to an army's roar

Breaking up in snaky swarms:

T   H

Torch and steel and snorting steed,

Hunted by the cry of blood,

Cursed with blindness, mad for day.

Where the torches ran a flood,

Tales of him and of the deed

Showered like a torrent spray.

Fear of silence made them strive

Loud in warrior-hymns that grew

Hoarse for slaughter yet unwreaked.

Ghostly Night across the hive,

With a crimson finger drew

Letters on her breast and shrieked.

Night was on them like the mould

On the buried half alive.

Night, their bloody Queen, her fold

Wound on them and struck them through.

　　Make the bed for Attila!

XXVII.

Earth has got him whom God gave,

Earth may sing, and earth shall smart!

None of earth shall know his grave.

They that dig with Death depart.

    Attila, my Attila !

XXVIII.

Thus their prayer was raved and passed :

Passed in peace their red sunset :

Hewn and earthed those men of sweat

Who had housed him in the vast,

Where no mortal might declare,

There lies he—his end was there !

    Attila, my Attila !

XXIX.

Kingless was the army left :

Of its head the race bereft.

Every fury of the pit

Tortured and dismembered it.

Lo, upon a silent hour,

When the pitch of frost subsides,

Danube with a shout of power

Loosens his imprisoned tides :

Wide around the frighted plains

Shake to hear his riven chains,

Dreadfuller than heaven in wrath,

As he makes himself a path :

High leap the ice-cracks, towering pile

Floes to bergs, and giant peers

Wrestle on a drifted isle ;

Island on ice-island rears ;

Dissolution battles fast :

Big the senseless Titans loom,

Through a mist of common doom

Striving which shall die the last :

Till a gentle-breathing morn

Frees the stream from bank to bank.

So the Empire built of scorn

Agonized, dissolved and sank.

Of the Queen no more was told

Than of leaf on Danube rolled.

Make the bed for Attila !

ANEURIN'S HARP

I.

PRINCE of Bards was old Aneurin ;

He the grand Gododin sang ;

All his numbers threw such fire in,

Struck his harp so wild a twang ;—

Still the wakeful Briton borrows

Wisdom from its ancient heat :

Still it haunts our source of sorrows,

Deep excess of liquor sweet !

II.

Here the Briton, there the Saxon,

Face to face, three fields apart,

Thirst for light to lay their thwacks on

Each the other with good heart.

Dry the Saxon sits, 'mid dinful

Noise of iron knits his steel :

Fresh and roaring with a skinful,

Britons round the hirlas reel.

III.

Yellow flamed the meady sunset ;

Red runs up the flag of morn.

Signal for the British onset

Hiccups through the British horn.

Down these hillmen pour like cattle

Sniffing pasture : grim below,

Showing eager teeth of battle

In his spear-heads lies the foe.

IV.

—Monster of the sea ! we drive him

Back into his hungry brine.

—You shall lodge him, feed him, wive him.

Look on us ; we stand in line.

—Pale sea-monster ! foul the waters

Cast him ; foul he leaves our land.

—You shall yield us land and daughters :

Stay the tongue, and try the hand.

V.

Swift as torrent-streams our warriors,

Tossing torrent lights, find way ;

Burst the ridges, crowd the barriers,

Pierce them where the spear-heads play ;

Turn them as the clods in furrow,

Top them like the leaping foam ;

Sorrow to the mother, sorrow,

Sorrow to the wife at home !

VI.

Stags, they butted ; bulls, they bellowed ;

Hounds, we baited them ; oh, brave !

Every second man, unfellowed,

Took the strokes of two, and gave.

Bare as hop-stakes in November's

Mists they met our battle-flood :

Hoary-red as Winter's embers

Lay their dead lines done in blood.

VII.

Thou, my Bard, didst hang thy lyre in

Oak-leaves, and with crimson brand

Rhythmic fury spent, Aneurin ;

Songs the churls could understand :

Thrumming on their Saxon sconces

Straight, the invariable blow,

Till they snorted true responses.

Ever thus the Bard they know !

VIII.

But ere nightfall, harper lusty!

When the sun was like a ball

Dropping on the battle dusty,

What was yon discordant call?

Cambria's old metheglin demon

Breathed against our rushing tide;

Clove us midst the threshing seamen :—

Gashed, we saw our ranks divide!

IX.

Britain then with valedictory

Shriek veiled off her face and knelt.

Full of liquor, full of victory,

Chief on chief old vengeance dealt.

Backward swung their hurly-burly;

None but dead men kept the fight.

They that drink their cup too early,

Darkness they shall see ere night.

X.

Loud we heard the yellow rover

Laugh to sleep, while we raged thick,

Thick as ants the ant-hill over,

Asking who has thrust the stick.

Lo, as frogs that Winter cumbers

Meet the Spring with stiffen'd yawn,

We from our hard night of slumbers,

Marched into the bloody dawn.

XI.

Day on day we fought, though shattered';

Pushed and met repulses sharp,

Till our Raven's plumes were scattered :

All, save old Aneurin's harp.

Hear it wailing like a mother

O'er the strings of children slain !

He in one tongue, in another,

Alien, I ; one blood, yet twain.

XII.

Old Aneurin ! droop no longer.

That squat ocean-scum, we own,

Had fine stoutness, made us stronger,

Brought us much-required backbone :

Claimed of Power their dues, and granted

Dues to Power in turn, when rose

Mightier rovers ; they that planted

Sovereign here the Norman nose.

XIII.

Glorious men, with heads of eagles,

Chopping arms, and cupboard lips ;

Warriors, hunters, keen as beagles,

Mounted aye on horse or ships.

Active, being hungry creatures ;

Silent, having nought to say :

High they raised the lord of features,

Saxon-worshipped to this day.

XIV.

Hear its deeds, the great recital!

Stout as bergs of Arctic ice

Once it led, and lived ; a title

Now it is, and names its price.

This our Saxon brothers cherish :

This, when by the worth of wits

Lands are reared aloft, or perish,

Sole illumes their lucre-pits.

XV.

Know we not our wrongs, unwritten

Though they be, Aneurin ?   Sword,

Song, and subtle mind, the Briton

Brings to market, all ignored.

'Gainst the Saxon's bone impinging,

Still is our Gododin played ;

Shamed we see him humbly cringing

In a shadowy nose's shade.

XVI.

Bitter is the weight that crushes

Low, my Bard, thy race of fire.

Here no fair young future blushes

Bridal to a man's desire.

Neither chief, nor aim, nor splendour

Dressing distance, we perceive

Neither honour, nor the tender

Bloom of promise, morn or eve

XVII.

Joined we are; a tide of races

Rolled to meet a common fate;

England clasps in her embraces

Many: what is England's state?

England her distended middle

Thumps with pride as Mammon's wife;

Says that thus she reads thy riddle,

Heaven! 'tis heaven to plump her life.

XVIII.

O my Bard ! a yellow liquor,

Like to that we drank of old—

Gold is her metheglin beaker,

She destruction drinks in gold.

Warn her, Bard, that Power is pressing

Hotly for his dues this hour ;

Tell her that no drunken blessing

Stops the onward march of Power.

XIX.

Has she ears to take forewarnings

She will cleanse her of her stains,

Feed and speed for braver mornings

Valorously the growth of brains.

Power, the hard man knit for action,

Reads each nation on the brow.

Cripple, fool, and petrifaction,

Fall to him—are falling now !

FRANCE, December 1870

I.

WE look for her that sunlike stood

Upon the forehead of our day,

An orb of nations, radiating food

For body and for mind alway.

Where is the Shape of glad array ;

The nervous hands, the front of steel,

The clarion tongue ?   Where is the bold proud face ?

We see a vacant place ;

We hear an iron heel.

II.

O she that made the brave appeal

For manhood when our time was dark,

And from our fetters drove the spark

Which was as lightning to reveal

New seasons, with the swifter play

Of pulses, and benigner day;

She that divinely shook the dead

From living man; that stretched ahead

Her resolute forefinger straight,

And marched toward the gloomy gate

Of earth's Untried, gave note, and in

The good name of Humanity

Called forth the daring vision! she,

She likewise half corrupt of sin,

Angel and Wanton! can it be?

Her star has foundered in eclipse,

The shriek of madness on her lips;

Shreds of her, and no more, we see.

There is horrible convulsion, smothered din,

As of one that in a grave-cloth struggles to be free.

III.

Look not for spreading boughs

On the riven forest tree.

Look down where deep in blood and mire

Black thunder plants his feet and ploughs

The soil for ruin : that is France :

Still thrilling like a lyre,

Amazed to shivering discord from a fall

Sudden as that the lurid hosts recall

Who met in heaven the irreparable mischance.

O that is France !

The brilliant eyes to kindle bliss,

The shrewd quick lips to laugh and kiss,

Breasts that a sighing world inspire,

And laughter-dimpled countenance

Where soul and senses caught desire !

IV.

Ever invoking fire from heaven, the fire

Has grasped her, unconsumeable, but framed

For all the ecstasies of suffering dire.

Mother of Pride, her sanctuary shamed :

Mother of Delicacy, and made a mark

T   I

For outrage : Mother of Luxury, stripped stark :

Mother of Heroes, bondsmen : thro' the rains,

Across her boundaries, lo the league-long chains !

Fond Mother of her martial youth ; they pass,

Are spectres in her sight, are mown as grass !

Mother of Honour, and dishonoured : Mother

Of Glory, she condemned to crown with bays

Her victor, and be fountain of his praise.

Is there another curse ?   There is another :

Compassionate her madness : is she not

Mother of Reason ? she that sees them mown

Like grass, her young ones !   Yea, in the low groan

And under the fixed thunder of this hour

Which holds the animate world in one foul blot

Tranced circumambient while relentless Power

Beaks at her heart and claws her limbs down-thrown,

She, with the plunging lightnings overshot,

With madness for an armour against pain,

With milkless breasts for little ones athirst,

And round her all her noblest dying in vain,

Mother of Reason is she, trebly cursed,

To feel, to see, to justify the blow ;

Chamber to chamber of her sequent brain

Gives answer of the cause of her great woe,

Inexorably echoing thro' the vaults,

' 'Tis thus they reap in blood, in blood who sow :

' This is the sum of self-absolvëd faults.'

Doubt not that thro' her grief, with sight supreme,

Thro' her delirium and despair's last dream,

Thro' pride, thro' bright illusion and the brood

Bewildering of her various Motherhood,

The high strong light within her, tho' she bleeds,

Traces the letters of returned misdeeds.

She sees what seed long sown, ripened of late,

Bears this fierce crop ; and she discerns her fate

From origin to agony, and on

As far as the wave washes long and wan

Off one disastrous impulse : for of waves

Our life is, and our deeds are pregnant graves

Blown rolling to the sunset from the dawn.

V.

Ah, what a dawn of splendour, when her sowers

Went forth and bent the necks of populations,

And of their terrors and humiliations

Wove her the starry wreath that earthward lowers

Now in the figure of a burning yoke !

Her legions traversed North and South and East,

Of triumph they enjoyed the glutton's feast :

They grafted the green sprig, they lopped the oak.

They caught by the beard the tempests, by the scalp

The icy precipices, and clove sheer through

The heart of horror of the pinnacled Alp,

Emerging not as men whom mortals knew.

They were the earthquake and the hurricane,

The lightnings and the locusts, plagues of blight,

Plagues of the revel : they were Deluge rain,

And dreaded Conflagration ; lawless Might.

Death writes a reeling line along the snows,

Where under frozen mists they may be tracked,

Who men and elements provoked to foes,

And Gods: they were of God and Beast compact:

Abhorred of all.   Yet, how they sucked the teats

Of Carnage, thirsty issue of their dam,

Whose eagles, angrier than their oriflamme,

Flushed the vext earth with blood, green earth forgets.

The gay young generations mask her grief;

Where bled her children hangs the loaded sheaf.

Forgetful is green earth; the Gods alone

Remember everlastingly: they strike

Remorselessly, and ever like for like.

By their great memories the Gods are known.

VI.

They are with her now, and in her ears, and known.

'Tis they that cast her to the dust for Strength,

Their slave, to feed on her fair body's length,

That once the sweetest and the proudest shone;

Scoring for hideous dismemberment

Her limbs, as were the anguish-taking breath

Gone out of her in the insufferable descent

From her high chieftainship ; as were she death,

Who hears a voice of justice, feels the knife

Of torture, drinks all ignominy of life.

They are with her, and the painful Gods might weep,

If ever rain of tears came out of heaven

To flatter Weakness and bid Conscience sleep,

Viewing the woe of this Immortal, driven

For the soul's life to drain the maddening cup

Of her own children's blood implacably :

Unsparing even as they to furrow up

The yellow land to likeness of a sea :

The bountiful fair land of vine and grain,

Of wit and grace and ardour, and strong roots,

Fruits perishable, imperishable fruits ;

Furrowed to likeness of the dim grey main

Behind the black obliterating cyclone.

VII.

Behold, the Gods are with her, and are known.

Whom they abandon misery persecutes

No more : them half-eyed apathy may loan

The happiness of pitiable brutes.

Whom the just Gods abandon have no light,

No ruthless light of introspective eyes

That in the midst of misery scrutinize

The heart and its iniquities outright.

They rest, they smile and rest ; have earned perchance

Of ancient service quiet for a term ;

Quiet of old men dropping to the worm ;

And so goes out the soul.   But not of France.

She cries for grief, and to the Gods she cries,

For fearfully their loosened hands chastize,

And icily they watch the rod's caress

Ravage her flesh from scourges merciless,

But she, inveterate of brain, discerns

That Pity has as little place as Joy

Among their roll of gifts ; for Strength she yearns,

For Strength, her idol once, too long her toy.

Lo, Strength is of the plain root-Virtues born :

Strength shall ye gain by service, prove in scorn,

Train by endurance, by devotion shape.

Strength is not won by miracle or rape.

It is the offspring of the modest years,

The gift of sire to son, thro' those firm laws

Which we name Gods ; which are the righteous cause,

The cause of man, and manhood's ministers.

Could France accept the fables of her priests,

Who blest her banners in this game of beasts,

And now bid hope that heaven will intercede

To violate its laws in her sore need,

She would find comfort in their opiates :

Mother of Reason ! can she cheat the Fates ?

Would she, the champion of the open mind,

The Omnipotent's prime gift—the gift of growth—

Consent even for a night-time to be blind,

And sink her soul on the delusive sloth,

For fruits ethereal and material, both,

In peril of her place among mankind ?

The Mother of the many Laughters might

Call one poor shade of laughter in the light

Of her unwavering lamp to mark what things

The world puts faith in, careless of the truth :

What silly puppet-bodies danced on strings,

Attached by credence, we appear in sooth,

Demanding intercession, direct aid,

When the whole tragic tale hangs on a broken blade !

She swung the sword for centuries ; in a day

It slipped her, like a stream cut off from source.

She struck a feeble hand, and tried to pray,

Clamoured of treachery, and had recourse

To drunken outcries in her dream that Force

Needed but hear her shouting to obey.

Was she not formed to conquer ?   The bright plumes

Of crested vanity shed graceful nods :

Transcendent in her foundries, Arts and looms,

Had France to fear the vengeance of the Gods ?

Her faith was on her battle-roll of names

Sheathed in the records of old war ; with dance

And song she thrilled her warriors and her dames,

Embracing her Dishonourer : gave him France

From head to foot, France present and to come,

So she might hear the trumpet and the drum—

Bellona and Bacchante ! rushing forth

On yon stout marching Schoolmen of the North.

Inveterate of brain, well knows she why

Strength failed her, faithful to himself the first :

Her dream is done, and she can read the sky,

And she can take into her heart the worst

Calamity to drug the shameful thought

Of days that made her as the man she served,

A name of terror, but a thing unnerved :

Buying the trickster, by the trickster bought,

She for dominion, he to patch a throne.

VIII.

Henceforth of her the Gods are known,

Open to them her breast is laid.

Inveterate of brain, heart-valiant,

Never did fairer creature pant

Before the altar and the blade !

IX.

Swift fall the blows, and men upbraid,

And friends give echo blunt and cold,

The echo of the forest to the axe.

Within her are the fires that wax

For resurrection from the mould.

X.

She snatched at heaven's flame of old,

And kindled nations : she was weak :

Frail sister of her heroic prototype,

The Man ; for sacrifice unripe,

She too must fill a Vulture's beak.

Deride the vanquished, and acclaim

The conqueror, who stains her fame,

Still the Gods love her, for that of high aim

Is this good France, the bleeding thing they stripe.

XI.

She shall rise worthier of her prototype

Thro' her abasement deep ; the pain that runs

From nerve to nerve some victory achieves.

They lie like circle-strewn soaked Autumn-leaves

Which stain the forest scarlet, her fair sons !

And of their death her life is : of their blood

From many streams now urging to a flood,

No more divided, France shall rise afresh.

Of them she learns the lesson of the flesh :—

The lesson writ in red since first Time ran

A hunter hunting down the beast in man :

That till the chasing out of its last vice,

The flesh was fashioned but for sacrifice.

Immortal Mother of a mortal host !

Thou suffering of the wounds that will not slay,

Wounds that bring death but take not life away !—

Stand fast and hearken while thy victors boast :

Hearken, and loathe that music evermore.

Slip loose thy garments woven of pride and shame :

The torture lurks in them, with them the blame

Shall pass to leave thee purer than before.

Undo thy jewels, thinking whence they came,

For what, and of the abominable name

Of her who in imperial beauty wore.

O Mother of a fated fleeting host

Conceived in the past days of sin, and born

Heirs of disease and arrogance and scorn,

Surrender, yield the weight of thy great ghost,

Like wings on air, to what the heavens proclaim

With trumpets from the multitudinous mounds

Where peace has filled the hearing of thy sons :

Albeit a pang of dissolution rounds

Each new discernment of the undying ones,

Do thou stoop to these graves here scattered wide

Along thy fields, as sunless billows roll ;

These ashes have the lesson for the soul.

' Die to thy Vanity, and strain thy Pride,

Strip off thy Luxury: that thou may'st live,

Die to thyself,' they say, 'as we have died

From dear existence, and the foe forgive,

Nor pray for aught save in our little space

To warm good seed to greet the fair earth's face.'

O Mother! take their counsel, and so shall

The broader world breathe in on this thy home,

Light clear for thee the counter-changing dome,

Strength give thee, like an ocean's vast expanse

Off mountain cliffs, the generations all,

Not whirling in their narrow rings of foam,

But as a river forward.   Soaring France!

Now is Humanity on trial in thee:

Now may'st thou gather humankind in fee:

Now prove that Reason is a quenchless scroll;

Make of calamity thine aureole,

And bleeding lead us thro' the troubles of the sea.

MEN AND MAN

I.

MEN the Angels eyed ;

And here they were wild waves,

And there as marsh descried,

Men the Angels eyed,

And liked the picture best

Where they were greenly dressed

In brotherhood of graves.

II.

Man the Angels marked : ·

He led a host through murk,

On fearful seas embarked,

Man the Angels marked ;

To think without a nay,

That he was good as they,

And help him at his work.

III.

Man and Angels, ye

A sluggish fen shall drain,

Shall quell a warring sea.

Man and Angels, ye,

Whom stain of strife befouls,

A light to kindle souls

Bear radiant in the stain.

THE LAST CONTENTION

I.

YOUNG captain of a crazy bark !

O tameless heart in battered frame !

Thy sailing orders have a mark,

    And hers is not the name.

II.

For action all thine iron clanks

In cravings for a splendid prize ;

Again to race or bump thy planks

    With any flag that flies.

T   K

III.

Consult them ; they are eloquent

For senses not inebriate.

They trust thee on the star intent,

    That leads to land their freight.

IV.

And they have known thee high peruse

The heavens, and deep the earth, till thou

Didst into the flushed circle cruise

    Where reason quits the brow.

V.

Thou animatest ancient tales,

To prove our world of linear seed :

Thy very virtue now assails,

    A tempter to mislead.

VI.

But thou hast answer : I am I ;

My passion hallows, bids command :

And she is gracious, she is nigh :

    One motion of the hand !

VII.

It will suffice ; a whirly tune

These winds will pipe, and thou perform

The nodded part of pantaloon

    In thy created storm.

VIII.

Admires thee Nature with much pride ;

She clasps thee for a gift of morn,

Till thou art set against the tide,

    And then beware her scorn.

IX.

Sad issue, should that strife befall

Between thy mortal ship and thee !

It writes the melancholy scrawl

    Of wreckage over sea.

X.

This lady of the luting tongue,

The flash in darkness, billow's grace,

For thee the worship ; for the young

    In muscle the embrace.

XI.

Soar on thy manhood clear from those

Whose toothless Winter claws at May,

And take her as the vein of rose

Athwart an evening grey.

PERIANDER

I.

How died Melissa none dares shape in words.

A woman who is wife despotic lords

Count faggot at the question, Shall she live !

Her son, because his brows were black of her,

Runs barking for his bread, a fugitive,

And Corinth frowns on them that feed the cur.

II.

There is no Corinth save the whip and curb

Of Corinth, high Periander ; the superb

In magnanimity, in rule severe.

Up on his marble fortress-tower he sits,

The city under him ; a white yoked steer,

That bears his heart for pulse, his head for wits.

III.

Bloom of the generous fires of his fair Spring

Still coloured him when men forbore to sting ;

Admiring meekly where the ordered seeds

Of his good sovereignty showed gardens trim ;

And owning that the hoe he struck at weeds

Was author of the flowers raised face to him.

IV.

His Corinth, to each mood subservient
In homage, made he as an instrument
To yield him music with scarce touch of stops.
He breathed, it piped ; he moved, it rose to fly :
At whiles a bloodhorse racing till it drops ;
At whiles a crouching dog, on him all eye.

V.

His wisdom men acknowledged ; only one,
The creature, issue of him, Lycophron,
That rebel with his mother in his brows,
Contested : such an infamous would foul
Pirene ! Little heed where he might house
The prince gave, hearing : so the fox, the owl !

VI.

To prove the Gods benignant to his rule,

The years, which fasten rigid whom they cool,

Reviewing, saw him hold the seat of power.

A grey one asked: Who next? nor answer had:

One greyer pointed on the pallid hour

To come: a river dried of waters glad.

VII.

For which of his male issue promised grip

To stride yon people, with the curb and whip?

This Lycophron! he sole, the father like,

Fired prospect of a line in one strong tide,

By right of mastery; stern will to strike;

Pride to support the stroke: yea, Godlike pride!

VIII.

Himself the prince beheld a failing fount.

His line stretched back unto its holy mount :

The thirsty onward waved for him no sign.

Then stood before his vision that hard son.

The seizure of a passion for his line

Impelled him to the path of Lycophron.

IX.

The youth was tossing pebbles in the sea ;

A figure shunned along the busy quay,

Perforce of the harsh edict for who dared

Address him outcast.   Naming it, he crossed

His father's look with look that proved them paired

For stiffness, and another pebble tossed.

X.

An exile to the Island ere nightfall

He passed from sight, from the hushed mouths of all.

It had resemblance to a death : and on,

Against a coast where sapphire shattered white,

The seasons rolled like troops of billows blown

To spraymist.   The prince gazed on capping night.

XI.

Deaf Age spake in his ear with shouts : Thy son !

Deep from his heart Life raved of work not done.

He heard historic echoes moan his name,

As of the prince in whom the race had pause ;

Till Tyranny paternity became,

And him he hated loved he for the cause.

XII.

Not Lycophron the exile now appeared,

But young Periander, from the shadow cleared,

That haunted his rebellious brows.   The prince

Grew bright for him ; saw youth, if seeming loth,

Return : and of pure pardon to convince,

Despatched the messenger most dear with both.

XIII.

His daughter, from the exile's Island home,

Wrote, as a flight of halcyons o'er the foam,

Sweet words : her brother to his father bowed ;

Accepted his peace-offering, and rejoiced.

To bring him back a prince the father vowed,

Commanded man the oars, the white sails hoist.

XIV.

He waved the fleet to strain its westward way

On to the sea-hued hills that crown the bay:

Soil of those hospitable islanders

Whom now his heart, for honour to his blood,

Thanked.   They should learn what boons a prince confers

When happiness enjoins him gratitude !

XV.

In watch upon the offing, worn with haste

To see his youth revived, and, close embraced,

Pardon who had subdued him, who had gained

Surely the stoutest battle between two

Since Titan pierced by young Apollo stained

Earth's breast, the prince looked forth, himself looked
     through.

XVI.

Errors aforetime unperceived were bared,

To be by his young masterful repaired :

Renewed his great ideas gone to smoke ;

His policy confirmed amid the surge

Of States and people fretting at his yoke.

And lo, the fleet brown-flocked on the sea-verge !

XVII.

Oars pulled : they streamed in harbour ; without cheer

For welcome shadowed round the heaving bier.

They, whose approach in such rare pomp and stress

Of numbers the free islanders dismayed

At Tyranny come masking to oppress,

Found Lycophron this breathless, this lone-laid.

XVIII.

Who smote the man thrown open to young joy?

The image of the mother of his boy

Came forth from his unwary breast in wreaths,

With eyes.   And shall a woman, that extinct,

Smite out of dust the Powerful who breathes?

Her loved the son ; her served ; they lay close-linked !

XIX.

Dead was he, and demanding earth.   Demand

Sharper for vengeance of an instant hand,

The Tyrant in the father heard him cry,

And raged a plague ; to prove on free Hellenes

How prompt the Tyrant for the Persian dye ;

How black his Gods behind their marble screens.

SOLON

I.

THE Tyrant passed, and friendlier was his eye
On the great man of Athens, whom for foe
He knew, than on the sycophantic fry
That broke as waters round a galley's flow,
Bubbles at prow and foam along the wake.
Solidity the Thunderer could not shake,
Beneath an adverse wind still stripping bare,
His kinsman, of the light-in-cavern look,
From thought drew, and a countenance could wear

Not less at peace than fields in Attic air

Shorn, and shown fruitful by the reaper's hook.

II

Most enviable so ; yet much insane

To deem of minds of men they grow ! these sheep,

By fits wild horses, need the crook and rein ;

Hot bulls by fits, pure wisdom hold they cheap,

My Lawgiver, when fiery is the mood.

For ones and twos and threes thy words are good ;

For thine own government are pillars : mine

Stand acts to fit the herd ; which has quick thirst,

Rejecting elegiacs, though they shine

On polished brass, and, worthy of the Nine,

In showering columns from their fountain burst.

III.

Thus museful rode the Tyrant, princely plumed,

To his high seat upon the sacred rock:

And Solon, blank beside his rule, resumed

The meditation which that passing mock

Had buffeted awhile to sallowness.

He little loved the man, his office less,

Yet owned him for a flower of his kind.

Therefore the heavier curse on Athens he!

The people grew not in themselves, but blind,

Accepted sight from him, to him resigned

Their hopes of stature, rootless as at sea.

IV.

As under sea lay Solon's work, or seemed

By turbid shore-waves beaten day by day;

T   L

Defaced, half formless, like an image dreamed,

Or child that fashioned in another clay

Appears, by strangers' hands to home returned.

But shall the Present tyrannize us? earned

It was in some way, justly says the sage.

One sees not how, while husbanding regrets;

While tossing scorn abroad from righteous rage,

High vision is obscured; for this is age

When robbed—more infant than the babe it frets.

v.

Yet see Athenians treading the black path

Laid by a prince's shadow! well content

To wait his pleasure, shivering at his wrath:

They bow to their accepted Orient

With offer of the all that renders bright :

Forgetful of the growth of men to light,

As creatures reared on Persian milk they bow.

Unripe ! unripe ! The times are overcast.

But still may they who sowed behind the plough

True seed fix in the mind an unborn Now

To make the plagues afflicting us things past.

BELLEROPHON

I.

MAIMED, beggared, grey ; seeking an alms ; with nod
Of palsy doing task of thanks for bread ;
    Upon the stature of a God,
He whom the Gods have struck bends low his head.

II.

Weak words he has, that slip the nerveless tongue
Deformed, like his great frame : a broken arc :
    Once radiant as the javelin flung
Right at the centre breastplate of his mark.

III.

Oft pausing on his white-eyed inward look,

Some undermountain narrative he tells,

As gapped by Lykian heat the brook

Cut from the source that in the upland swells.

IV.

The cottagers who dole him fruit and crust,

With patient inattention hear him prate :

And comes the snow, and comes the dust,

Comes the old wanderer, more bent of late.

V.

A crazy beggar grateful for a meal

Has ever of himself a world to say.

For them he is an ancient wheel

Spinning a knotted thread the livelong day.

VI.

He cannot, nor do they, the tale connect ;

For never singer in the land had been

Who him for theme did not reject :

Spurned of the hoof that sprang the Hippocrene.

VII.

Albeit a theme of flame to bring them straight

The snorting white-winged brother of the wave,

They hear him as a thing by fate

Cursed in unholy babble to his grave.

VIII.

As men that spied the wings, that heard the snort,

Their sires have told ; and of a martial prince

Bestriding him ; and old report

Speaks of a monster slain by one long since.

IX.

There is that story of the golden bit

By Goddess given to tame the lightning steed :

A mortal who could mount, and sit

Flying, and up Olympus midway speed.

X.

He rose like the loosed fountain's utmost leap ;

He played the star at span of heaven right o'er

Men's heads : they saw the snowy steep,

Saw the winged shoulders : him they saw not more.

XI.

He fell: and says the shattered man, I fell:

And sweeps an arm the height an eagle wins;

And in his breast a mouthless well

Heaves the worn patches of his coat of skins.

XII.

Lo, this is he in whom the surgent springs

Of recollections richer than our skies

To feed the flow of tuneful strings,

Show but a pool of scum for shooting flies.

PHAÉTHÔN

ATTEMPTED IN THE GALLIAMBIC MEASURE

At the coming up of Phoebus the all-luminous charioteer,
Double-visaged stand the mountains in imperial multitudes,
And with shadows dappled men sing to him, Hail, O Beneficent !
For they shudder chill, the earth-vales, at his clouding, shudder to black ;
In the light of him there is music thro' the poplar and river-sedge,
Renovation, chirp of brooks, hum of the forest—an ocean-song.
Never pearl from ocean-hollows by the diver exultingly,
In his breathlessness, above thrust, is as earth to Helios.

Who usurps his place there, rashest ? Aphrodite's loved one it is !
To his son the flaming Sun-God, to the tender youth, Phaethon,
Rule of day this day surrenders as a thing hereditary,
Having sworn by Styx tremendous, for the proof of his parentage,
He would grant his son's petition, whatsoever the sign thereof.
Then, rejoiced, the stripling answered : 'Rule of day give me ; give it
    me,
'Give me place that men may see me how I blaze, and transcendingly,
'I, divine, proclaim my birthright.' Darkened Helios, his utterance

Choked prophetic : ' O half mortal !' he exclaimed in an agony,

' O lost son of mine ! lost son ! No ! put a prayer for another thing :

' Not for this : insane to wish it, and to crave the gift impious !

' Cannot other gifts my godhead shed upon thee? miraculous

' Mighty gifts to prove a blessing, that to earth thou shalt be a joy ?

' Gifts of healing, wherewith men walk as the Gods beneficently ;

' As a God to sway to concord hearts of men, reconciling them ;

' Gifts of verse, the lyre, the laurel, therewithal that thine origin

' Shall be known even as when *I* strike on the string'd shell with melody,

' And the golden notes, like medicine, darting straight to the cavities,

' Fill them up, till hearts of men bound as the billows, the ships thereon.'

Thus intently urged the Sun-God ; but the force of his eloquence

Was the pressing on of sea-waves scattered broad from the rocks
away.

What shall move a soul from madness ? Lost, lost in delirium,

Rock-fast, the adolescent to his father, irreverent,

' By the oath ! the oath ! thine oath !' cried. The effulgent foreseer
then,

Quivering in his loins parental, on the boy's beaming countenance

Looked and moaned, and urged him for love's sake, for sweet life's
sake, to yield the claim,

To abandon his mad hunger, and avert the calamity.

But he, vehement, passionate, called out : 'Let me show I am what
I say,

' That the taunts I hear be silenced : I am stung with their whispering.

' Only, Thou, my Father, Thou tell how aloft the revolving wheels,

' How aloft the cleaving horse-crests I may guide peremptorily,

' Till I drink the shadows, fire-hot, like a flower celestial,

' And my fellows see me curbing the fierce steeds, the dear dew-drinkers :
' Yea, for this I gaze on life's light ; throw for this any sacrifice.'

All the end foreseeing, Phoebus, to his oath irrevocable,
Bowed obedient, deploring the insanity pitiless.
Then the flame-outsnorting horses were led forth : it was so decreed.
They were yoked before the glad youth by his sister-ancillaries.
Swift the ripple ripples follow'd, as of aureate Helicon,
Down their flanks, while they impatient pawed desire of the distances,
And the bit with fury champed.   Oh ! unimaginable glories !
Unimagined speed and splendour in the circle of upper air !
Higher, higher than the mountains, than the eagle fleeing arrows !
Glory grander than the armed host upon earth singing victory !
Chafed the youth with their spirit súrcharged, as when blossom is
    shaken by winds,
Marked that labour by his sister Phaethontiades finished, quick
On the slope of the car his forefoot set assured : and the morning
    rose :
Seeing whom, and what a day dawned, stood the God, as in harvest
    fields,
When the reaper grasps the full sheaf and the sickle that severs it :
Hugged the withered head with one hand, with the other, to indicate
(If this woe might be averted, this immeasurable evil),
Laid the kindling course in view, told how the reins to manipulate :
Named the horses fondly, fearful, caution'd urgently betweenwhiles :
Their diverging tempers dwelt on, and their wantonness, wickedness,
That the voice of Gods alone held in restraint ; but the voice of
    Gods ;

None but Gods can curb.   He spake : vain were the words : scarcely
    listening,
Mounted Phaethon, swinging reins loose, and, 'Behold me, companions,
'It is I here, I !' he shouted, glancing down with supremacy ;
'Not to any of you was this gift granted ever in annals of men ;
'I alone what only Gods can, I alone am governing day !'
Short the triumph, brief his rapture : see a hurricane suddenly
Beat the lifting billow crestless, roll it broken this way and that ;—
At the leap on yielding ether, in despite of his reprimand,
Swayed tumultuous the fire-steeds, plunging reckless hither and yon ;
Unto men a great amazement, all agaze at the Orient :—
Pitifully for mastery striving in ascension, the charioteer,
Reminiscent, drifts of counsel caught confused in his arid wits ;
The reins stiff ahind his shoulder madly pulled for the mastery,
Till a thunder off the tense chords thro' his ears dinned horrible.
Panic seized him : fled his vision of inviolability ;
Fled the dream that he of mortals rode mischances predominant ;
And he cried, 'Had I petitioned for a cup of chill aconite,
'My descent to awful Hades had been soft, for now must I go
'With the curse by father Zeus cast on ambition immoderate.
'Oh, my sisters !   Thou, my Goddess, in whose love I was enviable,
'From whose arms I rushed befrenzied, what a wreck will this body
    be,
'That admired of thee stood rose-warm in the courts where thy
    mysteries
'Celebration had from me, me the most splendidly privileged !
'Never more shall I thy temple fill with incenses bewildering ;
'Not again hear thy half-murmurs—I am lost !—never, never more.

'I am wrecked on seas of air, hurled to my death in a vessel of flame!
'Hither, sisters! Father, save me! Hither, succour me, Cypria!'

Now a wail of men to Zeus rang : from Olympus the Thunderer
Saw the rage of the havoc wide-mouthed, the bright car superimpending
Over Asia, Africa, low down ; ruin flaming over the vales ;
Light disastrous rising savage out of smoke inveterately ;
Beast-black, conflagration like a menacing shadow move
With voracious roaring southward, where aslant, insufferable,
The bright steeds careered their parched way down an arc of the
    firmament.
For the day grew like to thick night, and the orb was its beacon-
    fire,
And from hill to hill of darkness burst the day's apparition forth.
Lo, a wrestler, not a God, stood in the chariot ever lowering :
Lo, the shape of one who raced there to outstrip the legitimate
    hours :
Lo, the ravish'd beams of Phoebus dragg'd in shame at the chariot-
    wheels :
Light of days of happy pipings by the mead-singing rivulets !
Lo, lo, increasing lustre, torrid breath to the nostrils ; lo,
Torrid brilliancies thro' the vapours lighten swifter, penetrate them,
Fasten merciless, ruminant, hueless, on earth's frame crackling busily.
He aloft, the frenzied driver, in the glow of the universe,
Like the paling of the dawn-star withers visibly, he aloft :
Bitter fury in his aspect, bitter death in the heart of him.
Crouch the herds, contract the reptiles, crouch the lions under their
    paws.

White as metal in the furnace are the faces of humankind :
Inarticulate creatures of earth, dumb all await the ultimate shock.

To the bolt he launched, ' Strike dead, thou,' uttered Zeus, very terrible ;
' Perish folly, else 'tis man's fate ; ' and the bolt flew unerringly.
Then the kindler stooped ; from the torch-car down the measureless
    altitudes
Leaned his rayless head, relinquished rein and footing, raised not a cry.
Like the flower on the river's surface when expanding it vanishes,
Gave his limbs to right and left, quenched : and so fell he precipitate,
Seen of men as a glad rain-fall, sending coolness yet ere it comes :
So he showered above them, shadowed o'er the blue archipelagoes,
O'er the silken-shining pastures of the continents and the isles ;
So descending brought revival to the greenery of our earth.

Lither, noisy in the breezes now his sisters shivering weep,
By the river flowing smooth out to the vexed sea of Adria,
Where he fell, and where they suffered sudden change to the tremulous
Ever-wailful trees bemoaning him, a bruised purple cyclamen.

NOTES

THEODOLINDA.

The legend of the Iron Crown of Lombardy, formed of a nail of the true Cross by order of the devout Queen Theodolinda, is well known. In the above dramatic song she is seen passing through one of the higher temptations of the believing Christian.

PHAETHON.

THE GALLIAMBIC MEASURE.

Hermann (*Elementa Doctrinae Metricae*), after citing lines from the Tragic poet Phrynichus and from the Comic, observes :

Dixi supra, Phrynichorum versus videri puros Ionicos esse. Id si verum est, Galliambi non alia re ab his differunt, quam quod anaclasin, contractionesque et solutiones recipiunt. Itaque versus Galliambicus ex duobus versibus Anacreonteis constat, quorum secundus catalecticus est, hac forma :

The wonderful ATTIS of Catullus is the one classic example. A few lines have been gathered elsewhere. The Laureate's BOADICEA rides

over many difficulties and is a noble poem. Catullus makes general
use of the variant second of the above metrical forms :

Mihi januae frequentes, mihi limina tepida :

With stress on the emotion :

Jam, jam dolet quod egi, jam jamque poenitet.

A perfect conquest of the measure is not possible in our tongue.
For the sake of an occasional success in the velocity, sweep, volume of
the line, it seems worth an effort ; and, if to some degree serviceable
for narrative verse, it is one of the exercises of a writer which readers
may be invited to share.

THE END

Printed by R. & R. CLARK, *Edinburgh*

www.ingramcontent.com/pod-product-compliance
Lightning Source LLC
Chambersburg PA
CBHW020010030726

47500CB00002B/526